P9-DND-804

Dinosaur Kisses

David Ezra Stein

CANDLEWICK PRESS

After being in an egg
for some time, Dinah hatched out.

There was so much to see and do.

She tried this . . .

STOMP!

and that . . .

CHOMP!

Then she saw a kiss.

She decided to try that next.

"I will kiss you!"

WHOMP!

"Whoops," said Dinah.

"I will kiss you!"

CHOMP!

"Whoops," said Dinah.

"I will kiss you!"

"This time, if I'm really, really careful and I only use my lips . . .

then I can do it!

But she ate him.

"Whoops," said Dinah. "Not good."

Dinah went back to her egg to think.

Then she heard a noise.

KRAK!

"Hello," said the baby.

Dinah said, "I will kiss you!"

"What's kiss?" said the baby.

Dinah said, "Kiss is this!"

CHOMP!

The baby said, "Kiss is this?"

STOMP!

"Kiss!"

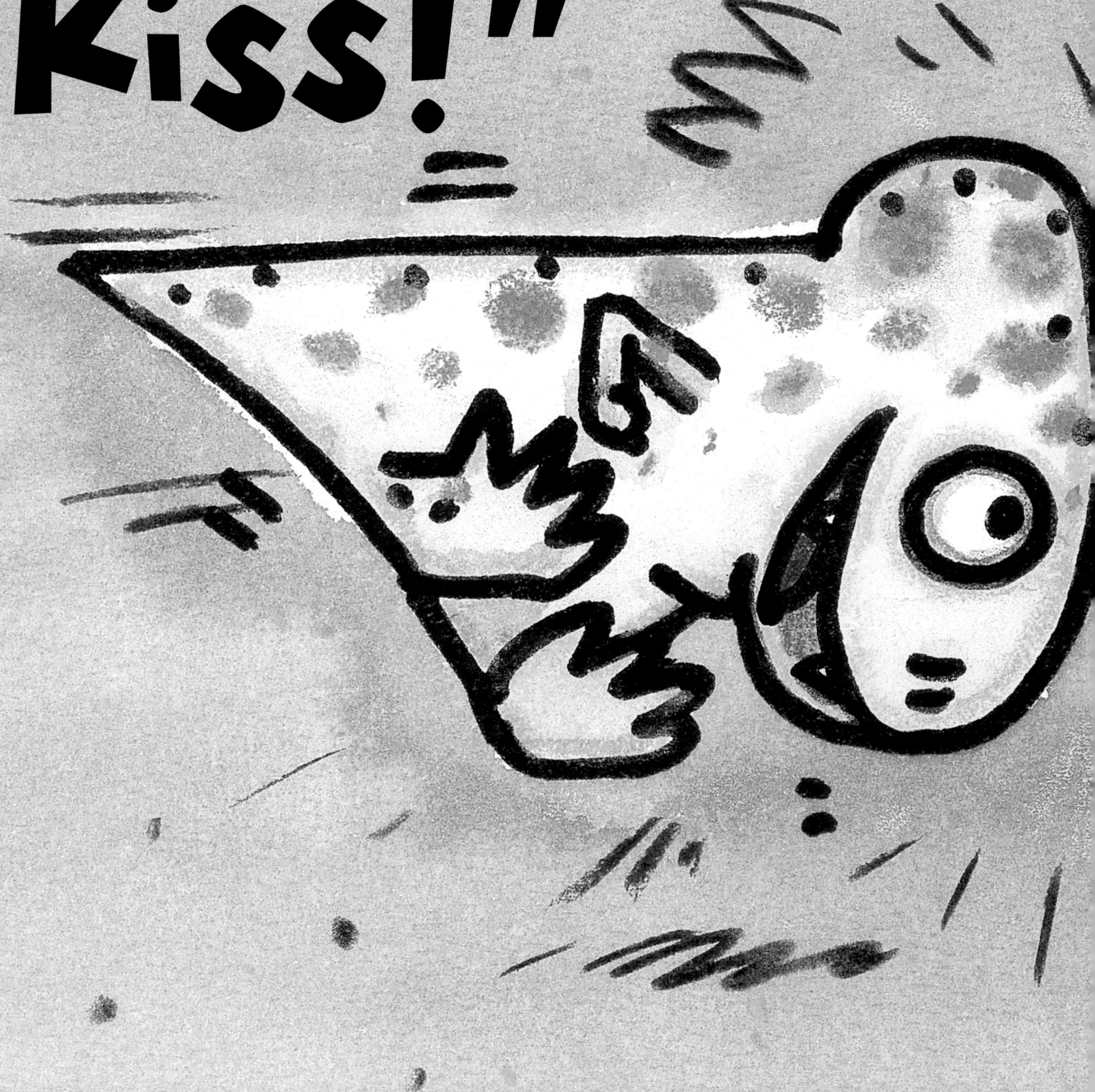